Thierry Dedieu made his English debut in 1993 with *The Little Christmas Soldier* (Henry Holt). Since then, he has written and illustrated dozens of books for children and has been published in multiple languages. Thierry lives in France. Visit his website at thierrydedieu.blogspot.com.

First published in the United States in 2019 by
Eerdmans Books for Young Readers,
an imprint of Wm. B. Eerdmans Publishing Co.
Grand Rapids, Michigan
www.eerdmans.com/youngreaders

Originally published in France under the title *Les bonshommes de neige sont éternels*.
© 2016 Éditions du Seuil
English-language translation © 2019 Eerdmans Books for Young Readers

Manufactured in China

27 26 25 24 23 22 21 20 19   1 2 3 4 5 6 7 8 9

Library of Congress Cataloging-in-Publication Data

Names: Dedieu, Thierry, author, illustrator.
Title: Snowmen live forever / by Thierry Dedieu.
Other titles: Bonshommes de neige sont éternels. English
Description: Grand Rapids, MI : Eerdmans Books for Young Readers, 2019. |
    Summary: When the Snowman disappears one spring, four animal friends set
    out to find their friend.
Identifiers: LCCN 2019003512 | ISBN 9780802855268
Subjects: | CYAC: Snowmen—Fiction. | Forest animals—Fiction. |
    Friendship—Fiction.
Classification: LCC PZ7.D35865 Sn 2019 | DDC [E]—dc23 LC record available at
https://lccn.loc.gov/2019003512

Snowmen Live Forever

thierry dedieu

eerdmans books for young readers

grand rapids, michigan

Early one morning, Squirrel (who was
always the first one out and about)
poked the tip of his nose out of the tree.

On his way down, he passed Owl, who had
just fallen asleep after a long night's watch.

"You can sleep when you're old!" said
Squirrel. "The others are on the way."

The others—Hedgehog and Rabbit—were already leaving their footprints in the fresh snow.

They all had an appointment with the
Snowman, and they did not want to miss him.
Every day for a month, they had spent
delightful days in his company.

The Snowman was better than anyone at organizing games, clowning around, thinking up riddles, and telling stories.

He seemed to know all the countries, and it was rumored that he had flown over India, the Americas, and Bhutan.

He could draw the winding Niger River from memory, describe every detail of the Khmer temples, and recount the birth of the northern lights.

But one day, this little world was shaken.

Squirrel made a disturbing discovery:
a crocus had just poked its way out of the
ground!

"I don't think he suspects anything," said Rabbit.

"Spring is coming, but he acts like everything is just fine," Hedgehog said.

"He wants to learn how to swim," said Owl.

"That's a little crazy, isn't it?"

The warmer it got, the more
strength the Snowman lost.

Until one day Squirrel found
the Snowman . . . almost
unrecognizable.

The sadness was short-lived, though.

At school, Master Bear taught Squirrel, Owl, Hedgehog, and Rabbit about how snow melts and water naturally flows from the mountains down to the sea.

Maybe they could find their friend!

"Onward!" cried Rabbit. "Let's go find the Snowman!"

"I'll bet that's why he wanted to learn to swim!" said Owl.

When they reached the seaside, they made a raft.
And then the four brave sailors set off to sea.

But after two days of searching, they hadn't seen a single trace of the Snowman. They were running out of food and water. It was time to head back to shore.

"We're looking for a drop of water in the big wide ocean!" said Hedgehog.

On the way back, a heavy silence hung
over the four friends, until suddenly . . .

"Look," said Squirrel. "Up there!"

"Hello, friends!" shouted the Snowman, sitting on a huge cumulus cloud.

"I have so many things to tell you! I flew over Tibet, I learned how to make a kite, and the clouds and the wind told me a legend about a great white tiger . . .

"When the first snowflakes fall, I'll be back!"